Liverpool Public Library
Employee Honor Roll

Cynthia Duryea

2005

PATRICIA POLACCO

The Graves Family
Goes Camping

Philomel Books

FOR THE GRAVES FAMILY, *the summer brought a familiar uneasiness. On this day, the very air was crackling with anticipation. A cold chill hissed along the floorboards of the house, sending the family spiders scampering for their webs. The fountain in the front garden spewed bloodred liquid as birds exploded in panicked flight from nearby trees, fleeing what seemed to be an unseen terror.*

"Oh, how lovely!" Shalleaux Graves exclaimed as she peered out of the kitchen window, surveying the gloom that shrouded the day. "A perfect summer day for our annual camping trip!"

Dr. Graves, knowing that it was nearly time to leave for the annual family camping trip, was desperately searching his shelves for just the right map. Now he climbed a tall ladder and pulled a dusty ancient scroll from the highest shelf. "Here it is!" he announced as he blew clouds of dust from the parchment and rolled it out on the desk.

Ronnie and his best friends, Seth and Sara, along with the family spiders, leaned over the map with great interest as Dr. Graves traced the map with his finger.

"There it is . . . Lake Bleakmire," he called out.

"And no one knows it's there but us, Dad?" Ronnie asked quietly.

"Almost no one," Dr. Graves answered, lost in thought. "Surrounded by a rocky escarpment with only one hidden tunnel leading through it, it is a place that time has forgotten. Untouched! A place legends are made of.

"Oh, children, just think what we might find there: new species of spiders, giant swamp leeches, even the warty *Toadus uglycus*. And," his voice dropped to a whisper, "perhaps creatures for which we have no names.

"But now, it's away to the car. We are ready to be under way," Dr. Graves announced, rolling up the map.

The tiny pink trailer stood waiting in the driveway, behind a car jammed with people and paraphernalia, as Dr. Graves checked off his list. "Foodstuffs and camping supplies?"

"We've got them," cooed Mrs. Graves.

"Dune buggies and sailboats!"

"Got them, too," Ronnie called out.

"Family spiders and bats on board?" Dr. Graves checked.

The quadruplets shook their heads in the affirmative.

"Summer guests?" Dr. Graves chortled as he peered in at Seth and Sara.

"Hurrah," they both answered.

"Scientific equipment?" he said, checking the last item on his list.

"You packed that yourself," Mrs. Graves answered.

"I feel like we have forgotten something!" Dr. Graves said thoughtfully.

"Phoebe!" everyone in the car shouted.

"Oh . . . of course . . . Phoebe!" Dr. Graves called out as he pushed the family's giant Venus flytrap and resident nanny into the car.

Just as the Graves' car pulled out of the driveway, Bill and Nancy Miller, Seth and Sara's parents, ran up to the car and leaned into the window.

"Now, you two mind Shalleaux, Phoebe and Dr. Graves," Mr. Miller said to the children. "Oh, and Doug, don't forget you have to be back a few days before the Fourth of July. The town council of Union City is expecting you to personally oversee setting up the fireworks."

"Not to worry, Bill," Dr. Graves called out, shifting into twelfth gear. "Tell Mayor Trenchmouth that, as always, I am in complete control. This will be the biggest Fourth of July show that Union City has ever seen. Trust me!"

Then, with a wave, Dr. Graves gunned out of the driveway. The little pink trailer tilted, a bevy of bats flying from its belfry, and the car sped off, leaving a trail of exhaust behind it. They were under way.

It was a long, hot drive, punctuated by taking the Irreversible Pass turnoff from 69 North, then crossing Pitfall Bridge, turning left at Longbowel Caves and chugging up Amputation Ridge, slogging over Harrowing Narrows and, finally, squeezing through the long escarpment tunnel that led into Dreadful Valley.

The forest got dark, dense and foul, only to open suddenly to threatening skies and a large murky lake.

"Bleakmire . . . ," Dr. Graves whispered, then bellowed, "we're here!" as the whole tribe piled out of the car.

Dr. Graves pushed a button on the console of the car. Seth and Sara stood back in utter amazement as the little pink trailer disconnected itself and shivered for a moment.

With that, the little pink trailer sprang into action. Awnings unfurled. The door swung open and belched out a fountain, an arbor and a fence with its own gate. A large picnic table shot out, along with assorted lawn chairs, a hammock and a swing. Then came a small boat, a barbecue pit, a stunning array of scientific equipment and finally, two garden gargoyles.

"Oh," cooed Mrs. Graves, patting them, "just like home! Now you children go inside, make your beds and wash up for lunch. Phoebe and I will have it ready in a jiffy."

Seth and Sara couldn't believe their eyes when they went into the little pink trailer. They were standing in a very large entry hall with marble floors. Then they walked into a great room with vaulted ceilings and a massive fireplace at the end. Just off from that room was a cavernous dining room with a table long enough to seat forty people.

Seth and Sara looked up at Ronnie.

"Don't ask," Ronnie said to them. "One of Dad's inventions. Something about bending space into an alternative continuum. He says he needs room for the specimens we'll be collecting."

After lunch of toasted Fijian jellyfish and strawberry malted eyeball milk, Dr. Graves and the children packed their backpacks and hiked out on their first expedition into Bleakmire Forest. They could hardly wait to go.

From the moment they stepped into the forest, the place looked like someplace they had never seen before.

"Positively prehistoric," Dr. Graves said as he took out his specimen case.

Seth and Sara had never seen spiders and snakes the size that they were seeing. On one particularly swampy bog, Seth stopped for a rest, unwrapping a sandwich for snack, and a slimy tongue whipped out of nowhere and grabbed his sandwich. He was face-to-face with the biggest, slimiest toad he'd ever seen.

Dr. Graves wrestled Seth's hand out of the *Toadus uglycus'* mouth and tucked the toad into his specimen case.

This was going to be the most amazing camping trip ever.

For the next two days, Dr. Graves and the children explored the night-time woods and slimy swamps of Bleakmire. They even took a small boat out to Queomich Island, a small island that changed its position in the lake with the tides.

And everywhere they collected gnashing knarps, Vernicious Knids, galloping bilge leeches and spotted tree splunkers. They filled every specimen bottle and basket Dr. Graves had brought, and filled up every other glass and container in Mrs. Graves' cupboard! Even her refrigerator and her dresser drawers! No question, Dr. Graves and the children were having the exploration of their lives.

Then, on the third day, Dr. Graves decided that it was time to explore the deepest, densest part of the forest.

The trees seemed to grow taller and taller, when all of a sudden, in the deepest, densest part, a very large furry spider slid down her silken web and stopped right in front of Dr. Graves' face.

"Hand me a specimen cage, Ronnie!" Dr. Graves called out.

But as Ronnie handed him the cage, Ronnie suddenly disappeared.

Seth and Sara jumped to where he was standing, and they disappeared, too. Dr. Graves stepped to see where they had all gone and he, too, vanished!

With a loud crash Dr. Graves landed just by the children. They had all fallen into a very deep hole! Dr. Graves looked up. The hole was too deep for any of them to climb out, even if they stood on each other's shoulders. There was no way out!

Suddenly a familiar face appeared above them.

"Phoebe!" Ronnie called out as she dropped a long rope to them.

Phoebe had saved the day, but when they'd all been pulled to safety, Dr. Graves bent to study the edges of the hole. "That was no ordinary hole," he said. "*That was an enormous footprint.*"

The children wheeled and looked. "But what could make a footprint like that?" Sara whispered.

Dr. Graves had no answer. But when they all got back to camp, Dr. Graves scoured his books on species, life-forms . . . and legends.

"By Jove . . . that's it!" Dr. Graves shouted with excitement. He was pointing at a fearsome picture of a hideous monster. "That is the footprint of the Flatulent Sulphuric Fermious Flying Griffin. A real fire-breather, the kind that legends are made of."

"You mean a fire-breathing dragon?" Sara said fearfully.

"But they don't exist . . . do they?" asked Seth fearfully.

"Of course not," said Dr. Graves. "At least, they are most certainly extinct now."

Before anyone could ask Dr. Graves anything more, though, Mrs. Graves called out, "Jum Jills, everyone!" and set out the most delightful little cake-like, muffinesque, cream-puffy, dream-puffy bite-sized morsels.

"Now, children, only one at a time. It won't do to eat these too fast!" Mrs. Graves said sternly.

Seth was first. He took one small bite, then uncontrollably stuffed the entire Jum Jill into his mouth.

"These are heavenly!" Sara gushed as she bolted one down with gusto.

"The best you've ever made, Lovie!" Dr. Graves added, smacking his lips.

"You have to give my mom the recipe," Sara said between mouthfuls.

"That isn't possible, my dear. You see, this recipe is a closely guarded family secret. Jum Jills have a very unusual effect on those who eat them—one bite and they go into a veritable eating frenzy!"

"Well, to bed, all. Tomorrow morning, we must away into the deepest, densest part of the forest again to study the footprint. This may be the scientific find of the century!" Dr. Graves said as he snatched one of the two Jum Jills left on the plate.

The next morning, the whole household awoke to the high-pitched screams of Mrs. Graves out by the campfire. Everyone raced outdoors, and they were stunned by what they saw.

"Footprints!" Ronnie said with alarm. "Exactly like the one we fell into."

"That means that that wasn't an ancient footprint," Seth said with even greater alarm. "These footprints are fresh. Just made!"

"A fire-breathing dragon here? Now?" Sara whispered.

Even Phoebe scampered into the little pink trailer and peered out, looking very concerned.

"Oh, dear!" Mrs. Graves gasped. "I understand. Someone left one single Jum Jill behind . . . and it looks like whatever this creature is ate it. But you all know what that means."

"IT WILL BE BACK FOR MORE!" everyone said in unison.

At exactly that moment, a dark shadow hovered above them. Then something swooped down out of the sky and landed with a watery crash that felled trees and swamped the shoreline. A horrifying screech came from it. A puff of acrid smoke and a plume of fire and brimstone arched from its mouth and burned a small thicket of trees to the ground.

Mrs. Graves pulled the children into the trailer.

"Wait!" Dr. Graves shouted as he picked up a piece of his scientific equipment. "My translanguageator!

"Let's see," he said as he fiddled with levers and buttons. "I'll set the base tongue at Lizard and Komodo Dragon, and hope that is close to its own language."

Then Dr. Graves set the machine on "project," lifted the announcing cone to his lips and called out a cheery, friendly greeting. The translanguageator whirred and popped and a sound rippled over the surface of the water and made trees flutter.

The creature cocked its head, narrowed its eyes and leaned close to the translanguageator, sniffing and snorting a puff of smoke.

"What does it want?" Mrs. Graves called out from the trailer.

Dr. Graves asked that very question into the projecting cone, then flipped a couple of switches. A strange sound came out of the machine that seemed to startle the creature. It came closer and bellowed back into the machine.

Dr. Graves flipped a couple of switches and a booming voice screamed, "FOOD!"

It wasn't long before the Graves family realized that the creature was interested in only one kind of food . . . Jum Jills!

In the next days, while Mrs. Graves, Phoebe and the children shoveled Jum Jills into the dragon as quickly as they could make them, Dr. Graves learned that the creature was the last of its kind, that it was a female, and that it was lonely. They also soon discovered that its appetite for Jum Jills was impossible to fill and that they were going to run out of supplies.

Then what? they wondered.

"We have to get back to Union City!" Mrs. Graves cried after a full day of the feeding frenzy.

"Bill and Nancy must be sick with worry, and the Fourth of July spectacular is only two days away!"

"I have a plan, Lovie. After the dragon's evening meal of Jum Jills, we'll break camp, drive up to the escarpment tunnel and leave," Dr. Graves whispered to his wife.

That evening, after the dragon flew off, the Graves family did exactly that. But when they got to the escarpment tunnel, the dragon was there waiting for them. It shrieked and spewed flames at the car, and stomped its feet so hard that it collapsed the tunnel, sealing them all in the valley.

Now there was no escape route.

But Mrs. Graves was angry. The next morning, Mrs. Graves was waiting for the creature. When it landed, she scolded into the translanguageator, "It would seem to me that you need to learn some manners! You make friends by being a friend, not holding people captive against their wills. You have frightened the children! Furthermore, any polite guest knows, when offered a basket of Jum Jills, a guest only takes one.

"And now you've trapped us here!" Mrs. Graves broke down and cried.

The dragon fluttered its eyes. Looking sheepish, it sniffed the basket of Jum Jills. Then it flew off, this time disappearing into the horizon.

All night, Dr. Graves was frantic. They had run out of food and supplies. He hadn't allowed cell phones on vacation, and they wouldn't have worked here anyway! They were trapped. And he was worried. What would happen when the dragon realized there were no more Jum Jills?

It was that moment when Dr. Graves noticed that Queomich Island seemed to be floating right toward the shore where he was sitting.

With a giant whoosh, it beached itself. It was only then that Dr. Graves noticed that it wasn't an island at all. It appeared to be a very large boat.

He set the entire family to pulling vines and brush off from the boat, and that's when he saw it silhouetted in the moonlight. It was the *Queen of Michigan*! Now he remembered a legend he had forgotten—that once there was a canal that connected this lake to streams and rivers and finally to the Great Lakes themselves. The *Queen of Michigan* had navigated that canal until the night of the Big Summer Storm nearly a hundred years before. That night, the riverboat had disappeared and had never been seen again. Nor had the canal!

"Lovie, it's our way out!" Dr. Graves exclaimed to Mrs. Graves. "Pack up the camp, drive the car and trailer onto the deck, and I'll look for a way to get the *Queen*'s engines to run again."

Dr. Graves filled the water tanks, and got the children to help him gather wood to stoke up the fires and get the boilers steaming. Then he dropped a small tablet into each water tank. "My own invention. It may give us a little boost when we need it," he said proudly.

When everyone was aboard, Seth stoked the fires, Sara pulled the steam valves, and Mrs. Graves steered while Dr. Graves freed the stern wheel. Then he and Ronnie read the ancient map. "According to this map, the entrance to the old canal is right about . . . there." He pointed at a mound of suspiciously tangled roots along the shore, not far from where they had camped.

"Full steam ahead!" he shouted, pointing at the spot.

With that, they got up a full head of steam and Mrs. Graves ran straight into what looked like the banks of Lake Bleakmire.

They spent a whole night navigating the canal, streams, rivers and finally a lake. Dr. Graves announced it was Union Lake, and their beloved Union City was dead ahead.

The riverboat bumped into shore at Shirt Tail Flutter, just across the St. Joe River from the football field where the fireworks show was going to happen in two short days. Ronnie looked up. "It looks like rain."

"Don't even think about it, son," Dr. Graves said.

"But what if it did rain? The fireworks would get wet, and that would be a disaster, wouldn't it?"

"Yes, but it isn't going to happen. Trust me," yawned Dr. Graves.
Exhausted from the night of travel, they drove the car and trailer home, and collapsed in their beds.

On the Fourth of July, Dr. and Mrs. Graves awoke to a commotion in their living room. "Mom, Dad," Ronnie was shouting. "It's the dragon. She followed us here! She's on the river next to the riverboat, right across from the football field!"

"Jum Jills," both Dr. and Mrs. Graves said.

"Doug, if that creature burns down the town with her breath, we most certainly will no longer be welcome in Union City!" Mrs. Graves sobbed.

But Dr. Graves was tapping his head. "Lovie, you best get busy making Jum Jills. It will buy time until I think what to do."

When they got to the river, the dragon had already pitched a temper tantrum, burned down a small clump of trees and thrashed about in the river so much that she had swamped the football field with water and soaked the fireworks!

"Naughty, naughty!" Dr. Graves scolded the dragon. It cowered low to the riverbank and looked sheepish. "I'll bring you some Jum Jills later tonight. You'll just have to wait!"

Dr. Graves spent most of that day racking his brain for a solution to the dragon problem. Not to mention how he was going to tell the whole town that the fireworks weren't happening.

"Here is the basket of Jum Jills, dear," Mrs. Graves said when she had made her first batch. Luckily Phoebe had helped. "Don't worry, people will understand about the fireworks."

Dr. Graves stared at the basket of Jum Jills for a moment, then he smiled wryly and took them to his laboratory in the basement. In a few moments, he came back upstairs, humming, and made his way to the riverbank, where he left the basket of Jum Jills.

That evening, the Union City High School Football Field was filled to capacity. As Dr. Graves climbed the steps to the platform, cameras crackled and people cheered, but as he stepped up to the microphone, he had a heavy heart. Clearly, his plan hadn't worked.

But just as he opened his mouth to announce that there would be no fireworks this year, something started to happen down on the riverbank across from the football field.

The ground rumbled and shook. Then there was an explosion of such monumental proportion that windows rattled in their panes as far away as Mackinac Island. Then, dazzling color shot into the night sky.

The crowd *ooooooohed* and *ahhhhhhhhed*.

Then there was a gargantuan, catastrophic burp that was so loud, it shattered vases clear over in Coldwater. More light and color catapulted up-up-up into the stratosphere. The lights were seen as far away as Mississippi!

Then a large balloon-looking thing darted around the sky, this way and that, with plumes of flame and fireworks shooting out of it.

Ronnie, Sara and Seth looked very carefully at the balloon. It was the dragon! It was wheezing and coughing flames and fireworks. It shot straight up with a belch, swooping down with a cough, and spiraled sideways with its stomach grumbling fiery puffs of rockets and color.

Oh, my, it was spectacular!

Well, sir, that Fourth of July was legendary, all right! That single night put Union City right up there with New York and Chicago in the annals of pyrotechnic displays. And there was no need at all for anyone to know that Dr. Graves had sprinkled his new and experimental firepower into those Jum Jills that night.

Of course, not a citizen, with the exception of the Graves and Miller families, would even learn of the dragon's existence. From that time on, she was content to stay quietly hidden in the marshes at Shirt Tail Flutter, next to the football field on the river. On some nights she was happy to take the Graves family, including Phoebe of course, out for a midnight flight on her leathery back. They had become quite good friends. They named her Barbara.

Of course, Mrs. Graves visited Barbara every morning and brought her a basket of Jum Jills. But she had learned her lesson. From that time on, she took only one Jum Jill. At least only one at a time.

To Wanda Gág and her funny thing
and to the Graves Family

Patricia Lee Gauch, Editor

PHILOMEL BOOKS   A division of Penguin Young Readers Group. Published by The Penguin Group.
Penguin Group (USA) Inc., 375 Hudson Street, New York, NY 10014, U.S.A.
Penguin Group (Canada), 10 Alcorn Avenue, Toronto, Ontario, Canada M4V 3B2 (a division of Pearson Penguin Canada Inc.)
Penguin Books Ltd, 80 Strand, London WC2R 0RL, England.   Penguin Ireland, 25 St. Stephen's Green, Dublin 2, Ireland (a division of Penguin Books
Ltd.)   Penguin Group (Australia), 250 Camberwell Road, Camberwell, Victoria 3124, Australia (a division of Pearson Australia Group Pty Ltd).
Penguin Books India Pvt Ltd, 11 Community Centre, Panchsheel Park, New Delhi - 110 017, India.   Penguin Group (NZ), Cnr Airborne and
Rosedale Roads, Albany, Auckland 1310, New Zealand (a division of Pearson New Zealand Ltd).   Penguin Books (South Africa) (Pty) Ltd, 24 Sturdee
Avenue, Rosebank, Johannesburg 2196, South Africa.   Penguin Books Ltd, Registered Offices: 80 Strand, London WC2R 0RL, England.

Published simultaneously in Canada. Manufactured in China by South China Printing Co. Ltd.
Design by Semadar Megged. Text set in 15-point Adobe Jenson. The art was done in pencil and watercolor.
Library of Congress Cataloging-in-Publication Data
Polacco, Patricia.   The Graves family goes camping / Patricia Polacco.   p. cm.   Summary: When the Graves family goes on their annual camping trip
to Lake Bleakmire, they make a frightening discovery in the forest. [1. Dragons—Fiction. 2. Humorous stories.] I. Title.   PZ7.P75186Gt 2005
[E]—dc22   2004018116   ISBN 0-399-24369-0
1 3 5 7 9 10 8 6 4 2
First Impression